This book belongs to . . . .

Ice Sausages

Fairy Cakes

Star Pie

Knickerbocker Glory

Fairydust Flan

Wibbly Wobbly Jelly

Banana Pizza

Splodgy Pudding

Funday Sundae

Jumping Jelly Beans

For Agnes

with thanks to Penny and Tiffany

EGMONT
We bring stories to life

First published in Great Britain 2008 by Egmont UK Limited
This edition published 2018 by Dean,
an imprint of Egmont UK Limited,
The Yellow Building, 1 Nicholas Road, London, W11 4AN
www.egmont.com

Text and Illustrations copyright © Sue Heap 2008
The moral rights of Sue Heap have been asserted

ISBN 978 0 6035 7565 5
70165/001
Printed in Malaysia

A CIP catalogue record for this title is available from the British Library

The FABULOUS FAIRY FEAST

by Sue Heap

EGMONT

One day in Fairyland, Lizzie Little-Fairy was riding her special pink bicycle and reading her favourite book when her pet frog, Burp, appeared with an invitation from the Fairy Queen.

The invitation read like this:

Dear Lizzie Little-Fairy

You are royally invited to a fabulous midnight feast tonight at the magical meeting place. Please bring your best pet.

The Fairy Queen

So Lizzie Little-Fairy put Burp in the basket of her special pink bicycle and off they went.

over a cloud

They cycled up into the sky,

The Woods

and down,

down, down, into . . .

THE WOODS!

Which is where they saw
all their friends!

Ellie and her elephant,
Kirsty and her cat,
Fiona and her fox,
Bertie and his bat.
Gloria brought her goose,
Henry brought a hen,
Betsy had her bear,
A rabbit was with Ben.
And Mark brought his shark
(who didn't like the woods
and didn't like the dark!)

And everyone loved
Lizzie's pink bicycle. They all wished
they could have a go on it!

At the arrival of the Queen,
all the fairies curtseyed and all the pets bowed.
"Welcome fairies and your pets," she said,
"to my fabulous midnight feast!"

Everyone clapped and cheered.
In all the excitement, Burp
hopped off Lizzie's head . . .

. . . and landed in the
Queen's bag, which
was being carried
by Maurice the Monkey . . .

. . . who thought it would
be funny to take it up into
the tallest tree!

a spare pair of wings

the right royal hankie,

Lizzie's frog Burp,

the Queen's magic wand,

As everyone looked up,
that mischievous monkey
tipped out the bag
and down fell . . . .

and all the wishing feathers

the Queen had brought along for later.

The wand's magic was let loose.

Ellie's elephant started dancing.

Fiona's fox began to fly.

They caused such havoc,

it made the shark cry.

Feathers sprouted on Rabbit. Ears grew on the goose.
Gloria and Ben now had a gabbit and a roose!

Henry's hen laid a pen.

Betsy's bear looked like a pear.

And Bertie's bat became Bertie

and Bertie became his bat.

How crazy is that?

said Kirsty's cat.

And just as midnight struck, Burp handed the Queen her lost wand, and Lizzie gave back all the things from her bag.

With a wave of the wand,
all the madness and muddling stopped.
"I declare it's midnight!"
said the Queen.
"Let the feast begin."

And everyone sat down to a FABULOUS

Wibbly Wobbly Jelly

Saucy Spaghetti

Jumping Jelly Beans

Ice Sausages

Early Grey Tea

Fairydus

FAIRY FEAST

Fizzy Fudge cake

Star Pie

Chocolate Chips

Banana Pizza

Splodgy Pudding

Knickerbocker Glory

Carrot!

When everyone had eaten and it was time to go home,
the Queen gave them all a wishing feather.
She told them to close their eyes
and make a wish . . .

. . . and everyone's wish came true!

Even Burp's!